# DADDY'S JOURNALS: An Intimate Journey Into Parenthood!
Written by K. Erickson Smith

Pa-Pro-Vi Publishing: www.paprovipublishing.com

*Dedication*

*First and foremost, I am so grateful to God and my Lord and Savior Jesus Christ for the opportunity to show His love for me in this book.*

*To my amazing wife Heather Hastings Smith, words cannot capture the joy and excitement I feel when I consider the value you have brought to my life through your boundless creativity. There is no story without you. For over twenty-five years, you poured your life out for this family. This book is our celebration for your sacrifice and unwavering love for me and the kids.*
*You are the best decision I have ever made.*

*To my two great joys, Kennedi and Myles. I am more than proud that God has allowed me to be your father. Fatherhood doesn't come with a manual but I hope and pray that you know that your mother and I love you and will support you as you enter young adulthood.*

*To the Smith, Hastings, Covin, and Pugh families...thank you for loving me and encouraging me to follow my purpose in life.*

*To my distinguished brothers of Alpha Phi Alpha Fraternity Incorporated (particularly the Zeta Pi and Rho Kappa Lambda chapters) in your endless pursuit for the betterment of mankind.*

*To the countless family members, godparents, godchildren, and friends who God has used to bless my family over the past 25 years, you were the answers to my prayers found in this book. You stepped up to complete our village and I am forever grateful for your love and support.*

*To the fathers and father figures whose intention always lean toward becoming the best version of themselves for their children.*

*To my late father Alexander Smith Sr. I give thanks for the wisdom you shared with me that I could not understand as a child. You challenged me to be great because you knew I had to be for Kennedi and Myles. Your spirit has been with me through it all. These thoughts are dedicated to you...my world.*
*Thank you.*

The family you could only conceptualize bearing in Mid-June 1997, has as of now been an over 23-year long journey of bonding, challenges, growth and fulfillment. Your will to create an empire has come to pass, and continues to unfold and transpire day to day. Your desires to raise children that are selfless and know God has been fulfilled. You've raised a very strong daughter and a very strong son, and if nobody else tells you, both are extremely proud of you. You decided you wanted to give two human beings life on this earth, and created yourself to be a vessel for two more parts of God's purpose in the world to be enacted. Each and every sacrifice that has been made on our behalf has been a gift-- a gift that will never go unnoticed. A gift that will serve so many people beyond yourself. A gift that will keep giving as long as I live, as long as Myles lives, and every subsequent generation after us that will only exist because of your mid-June 1997 desire. You passed to your daughter the ability to envision a goal and to work persistently towards it as you were the very first coach she's ever known. You passed to your daughter your analytical style of thinking as she has grown up over the years and has always been one to desire a deeper understanding of the things that she is passionate about. You passed to your daughter an image of God's love, as she has been able to see through you what it looks like to follow God unceasingly and to keep him in the core of her life.
Love you, Kennedi

# OUR FIRSTBORN CHILD

**Mid-June, 1997** – Your mother and I decided to start a family. Little did we know that the family would come so quickly.

**Wednesday, June 25** – Your mother's menstrual period began; it ended on the following Saturday (June 28th) – the night of the second Tyson-Holyfield fight. We had an impromptu fight party over at our house. The Bayonnes, Whites, Chris, Derrick, Auntie Lorraine (Mommy's sister), and others were there. Mike Tyson bit off a piece of Evander Holyfield's ear and was disqualified. He was later suspended from boxing for one year.

**Tuesday, July 15(?) – 3 weeks old** – I believe this was the day of conception. Your mother did not think so, but I knew from the beginning. I knew we had conceived a baby. We would probably disagree to this day about the day of conception but I'm certain that this was the day. Mid-July – Your mother complains of having acute smelling – early symptoms of pregnancy, but we did not know it at the time.

**Wednesday, July 30 – 5 weeks old** – Your mother and I were planning to take a weekend vacation to Daytona Beach when your mother noticed that she was slightly spotting. She figured that her menstrual period was coming, but we later realized you had simply attached yourself to her womb – this is called implantation. At this point, we did not think that your mother was pregnant.

**Thursday, July 31 – 5 weeks/ 1 day-** We stopped in Dublin on our way to Daytona to spend the night. Your Grandma Dot (my mother), was sleeping when we got there because she had to go to work at midnight. Usually we get a simply "hey, how ya'll doing?", but the first words that come out of her mouth were, "Are ya'll pregnant?" Although Heather was nearly two weeks late by this point, we dispelled the notion because of the spotting. But the spotting was very light and there was no flow by this point. Could it be that Heather is pregnant now? I didn't know but I wanted to wait at least another week before we took a test. Heather wanted to know as soon as possible because it was driving her nuts!

**August 1-3** (Daytona Beach) Although we tried to make the most out of the trip, your mother and I had a horrible time. We earned the trip by attending this timesharing presentation (we will explain to you later), We realized that they did not assign accommodations until the people get there. Baby, they put your parents in a run-down Days Inn that was so nasty, it makes the projects look like five-star condominiums. You should have seen your mother refusing to touch one thing in that place. It was so nasty!!! Your mother doesn't like hotels anyway, but this one was especially distasteful. We had fun on the beach but we refused to spend anytime in the room. The only reason why we stayed was because the trip was free. Otherwise, we would have been out of there. All weekend I would ask Boo (that's your mother) if her period had arrived. She would say no with this smirk on her face. Your mother's face was so clear. Usually she would have one little pimple in her face when her menstrual is to come, but no such thing. I figured it was a good chance she was pregnant but I was still uncertain. We definitely did not want to get one of those expensive over-the-counter pregnancy test just to find out that it was negative, so we decided to wait a little while longer. The suspense was killing both of us.

**Wednesday, August 6 – 6 weeks old** – Your mother decided to go to the doctor to have a pregnancy test. The appointment was at 2:00PM and I was nervous all morning but I really wanted your mother to be pregnant but I didn't want to be disappointed. Your mother teased me all day that she was not going to tell me until we got home, but I convinced her to call me when she got the results. At 2:45PM the phone rang. It was Heather. She told me that I would be a father, and I almost jumped out of my chair in disbelief. I'M GOING TO BE SOMEONE'S FATHER!!! My voice was three octaves higher than normal but I was so excited about the news. The nurse gave Boo a due date of April 4, but we later realized that your mother gave them the incorrect information concerning her last menstrual period (it would be later changed to March 31). We were so happy that soon we would have a bundle of love to claim as ours in the house.

**Tuesday, August 12 – 6 weeks/6 days** – Your mother's first morning sickness and it was not pretty.I felt so bad because I felt fine. The next morning, your mother could barely walk around without feeling like throwing up. For the next three days, Mama Mama (your mother) was sick from sunrise to sunset. Anything that she smelled that did not agree with her caused to her become sick. She missed work one day that week.

**Friday, August 15 - 7 weeks/ 2 days** - We visited Candice and Byron Campbell at Northside Hospital. They later delivered a baby boy, Kyle Christopher Campbell, on Sunday morning. I'm sure you will meet him one day.

**Friday, August 29 – 9 weeks/2 days** – Mama Mama has been sick off and on for more than two weeks now. Cooking has become difficult because the aroma triggers sickness. During sick period, she could only eat saltine crackers, honey grahams, ginger ale, and ice chips. Each week I try to make a fruit salad for her to eat.

**Tuesday, September 2 – 9 weeks/6 days** – It's our second wedding anniversary and we had our first doctor's appointment but we were somewhat disappointed because we didn't realize that they would only be taking personal history and not be giving your mother a physical. We didn't get to see you this time, but we knew you were still there because your mother was still throwing up. In fact, that night was a bad sickness night, and your mother laid on the couch all night. She felt so bad that she thought that she was about to die. She went to work late the next day. We have decided (for good) on your name – If you are a girl, it will be Kennedi Alexandria; if you are a boy, it would be Cameron Bryce. Aren't they beautiful names!! World News: Princess Diana of Wales died Saturday night in a tragic accident and the whole world is in shock.

**Saturday, September 6 -10 weeks/3 days** – We spent the night at your godparent's house (Uncle Dudley and Auntie Claire – they are also expecting your godbrother or sister). Mama Mama threw up again when she smelled breakfast cooking. When she felt better, we all went to Babies R Us where we fell in love with so much baby stuff. I told your mother that we should take a gamble on buying "girl" stuff and then bring it back if you were a boy. She did not go for that idea. We are not going to find out what sex you are but it sure is tempting.

**Tuesday, September 9 - 10 weeks/6 days** – We went to our first physical examination. The midwife informed me that I had to take a blood test to determine if I carried the sickle cell trait since your mother carried Hemoglobin AC which is a carrier trait. We took the test as a precaution, but we rebuked that notion in the name of Jesus. We knew you would be a healthy baby. We did not worry about it. We saw you for the first time today on the ultrasound because the midwife could not pick up your heartbeat on the Doppler. You are so tiny!!! You are about an inch long and you are lying on your back on the back wall of your mother's tummy. We saw your little heart beating and your legs wiggling. It was one of the most amazing things we had ever seen. One day you will become a human being living on this earth. It still has not hit us that you are coming. The midwife told us that we should be able to hear your heartbeat on the next visit.

**Wednesday, September 10 – 11 weeks old** – We talked to your grandmothers and they both want you to be a girl. We will see your Grandma Dot this weekend because we're going to my 10-year high school class reunion. Grandma Beryl definitely wants you to be a girl because she does not have a granddaughter. Grandma Dot has one but wants another. She said she has already seen you in her dreams. Makes me believe that you are indeed a girl. Your grandmother is seldom wrong. Your mother is feeling better but she has her moments. Please be gentle on her.

**Sunday, September 14 – 11 weeks/4 days** – Your mother is "showing" with you a little more each day. She looked in the mirror and started feeling fat, but your mother looks so pretty to me. It's great to watch you grow. Your mother ate baked beans, potato salad, and field peas all weekend at your Grandma Dot's house. Last week she ate nothing but red beans and rice that Grandma Beryl cooked. You think that's something? You wait until the Holiday Season … you're going to see a lot of food!!!

**Wednesday, September 17 – 12 weeks old** – Just when we thought we were out of the woods – Mama gets sick again. She threw up this morning after going to bed feeling uneasy last night. Baby, I hope you finish developing soon and starting to grow. Maybe then Mama can feel better about the pregnancy. I sung "Jesus loves me" to you last night. Did you like it? I will sing to you again later.

**Wednesday, September 24 – 13 weeks/5 days** – Congratulations, Baby!!! You're in the second trimester now. Your dad is in Chattanooga on business and misses you terribly. I know you miss me rubbing you... Don't worry .... I'll be home on Friday. Love ya.

**Monday, September 29 – 13 weeks/5 days** – Your mother and I were discussing daycare and the fact that we both are nervous about placing you with someone we do not know. We have talked about having your mother stay home with you for six months, but that will be a hard decision financially. We know that God has not forsaken us for anything and we do not expect Him to do so now. We will teach you that God is in control of all situations and now we will put our faith in Him to make sure that you are taken care of and that our financial needs are met. I claim in the name of Jesus that everything will be in place when you arrive. I don't know how but I do know it will happen. Baby, God does not forsake His children and we are His children – even you.

**Tuesday, September 30 – 13 weeks/6 days-** Just when I thought your mother was doing better, she throws up big time!!! She says that coughing causes her to throw up what's on her stomach. She was concerned about "what" she was throwing up and decided to call Prucare. When she called them they told her that they would find a nurse and call her back. It took them a half an hour to call back. Mom was falling asleep and I told her to go to bed. She said that she was waiting for their call, but I told her that they were not going to call. I'm sure glad it was not an emergency situation. When they finally called they basically brushed it off as a minor condition and told her to go to the doctor as a precaution. I think she and you are alright, but we cannot be too careful. You are too precious to us. By the way ... your Grandma Dot will be spending the night with us tomorrow. I'm taking her to the airport to see your Auntie Mel, Uncle Garf, and your cousin Jessica in Oklahoma. Tomorrow is also your cousin A.J.'s birthday. He will be 9 years old.

**Wednesday, October 1 – 14 weeks** – Mom felt her first cramps today. The midwife told us that this is due to the uterus stretching – that means you are growing!!! Mom also cannot stand to smell Dawn dishwashing liquid. She says it stinks. I can't wait until the 14th when Mom goes for her monthly visit. You should be a big boy or girl by then. Hopefully we will be able to hear your heartbeat this time. Mom's stomach feels much firmer than previous weeks. We sing in the choir this Sunday. This will be the first Sunday your mother has sung in the choir since June. I know she will be excited.

**Thursday, October 2 – 14 weeks/1 day** – Your mother and I are struggling with this issue of her always balling up and "cramping your style." I tell her that she needs to stretch out her legs to give you room, but she refuses to listen. I can't wait for the day when you're going to grow so much that she won't be able do it anymore. I'm just trying to look out for your best interest. Daddy won't let anything happen to his baby. I believe you like those rubs I give you at night. Daddy wants the baby to be comfortable in Mommy's tummy. You have a long way to go but God will bring you safely to us in good health.

**Saturday, October 4 -14 weeks/3 days** – Auntie Lorraine bought you a whole bunch of toys at a garage sale for your arrival. She bought a play pen, a baby walker, and a diaper genie to put your dirty diapers in. Auntie is also moving into a house in January and I'm sure she will decorate a room just for you. I guarantee she, your mother and your grandmothers will buy you plenty more before this pregnancy is over …. So just hold tight…. more goodies are on the way.

**Wednesday, October 8 – 15 weeks** – Wow!!! You're almost 4 months into the pregnancy. Anyone else would probably say that your mother is not showing with you, but she and I can feel the hard part of the stomach that we believe is the uterus (that's the place where you are growing inside your Mommy's tummy). We were playing with it tonight. When we poke it, it would move to the other side of your mother's stomach. We hope we didn't disturb your sleep or anything, but we're so excited about you that we cannot help ourselves. I might as well apologize ahead of time because we will probably poke you throughout this pregnancy …. Especially when you become larger and your movement become visible. Daddy and Mommy just want to make sure that you are alright in there. I put my ear to Mommy's stomach to hear what's going on down there. I hear a lot of "swishing noises – maybe that's the fluid that surrounds you in the womb. We can't wait until Tuesday when we receive our monthly checkup. Hopefully this time we will hear a heartbeat. I know Grandma Dot claimed that you would be a girl, but I'm still unsure. One minute I'm thinking about little girls; the next minute, little boys. Luckily I don't care – I just pray that you are healthy and sound. To let you know what's going on in the world while you're in there. The Braves beat the Marlins in Game 2 of the National League Championship Series to tie the series at one game a piece. The great Dean Smith just retired as University of North Carolina basketball coach.

**Sunday, October 12 – 15 weeks/4 days** – Your mother is losing her mind! Do you know that your mother just fussed me out for throwing away a pitcher of lemonade. See, we were expecting Shawn and Tracey Lacey (they're expecting a little boy next month) for dinner at 4:00. I wanted some Kool-Aid and we only have one large pitcher. So I threw out the lemonade that was in the pitcher and replaced it with Kool-Aid. Now your mother was about to have a fit because she loved that lemonade. She said I could have put the lemonade in another container and that is probably true, but I didn't want it anymore. Baby, it takes five minutes to make a pitcher of lemonade. Your mother didn't have to fuss like that. I hope she didn't scare you when she was hollering and screaming all over the house. To make a long story short, I finally made her lemonade, but she said that it did not taste like the first batch. Is this what pregnancy is all about? After the Lacey's left, Mommy was complaining about her stomach feeling tight. You must be down there trying to make room for yourself.

**Monday, October 13 – 15 weeks/ 5 days** – This has been a very stressful day so far for your mother. This morning her car broke down on Holt Road around 7:05 am. She waited for over twenty minutes hoping either your Grandpa Dan or I to come that way and see her off to the side of the road (we also go that way to work). Your mother was close to hysteria when she called. I thought she had been in an accident, but she told me that the car simply stopped after she turned onto Holt Road from S. Deshon Rd. When I got there about five minutes later, I pushed the car out of the roadway and took her back home. She didn't stop crying until we got home. We called your Uncle Andrew (Mommy's brother), to send a tow truck to take it to Aamco. At 10:30a.m. I called Uncle Andrew to see if the car had made it to the shop and he said it was on its way. Later, Uncle Andrew and your mother eventually called the store where the work was done (or not done) and told them that they should be responsible for the towing charges and any labor costs associated with repairing the car. Mommy said that they seemed receptive to that notion and told Uncle Andrew to inform them of the total costs. I just hope we can get our car by the end of the week. Mommy had to take Tylenol for the first time since she found out that she was pregnant. The Braves are down 3 games to 2 to the Marlins so I need you rooting for the Braves in there.

**Tuesday, October 14 – 15 weeks/6 days –** We went to have our routine visit to see how you are doing. We heard your heartbeat for the first time. It was beating at 148 beats a minute. Mommy's supervisor, Michelle, has a theory that whenever the baby's heart beat is higher than 140, it's a girl. Anything lower than that is a boy. You know that if you turn out to be a boy, Daddy will be so thrilled, but if you are a girl then no one will be able to use the name Kennedi for their child without being a copy-cat. That's selfish, isn't it? I know but Daddy wants your name to be special because you are special to us. Your Mommy and Daddy pray for you every night that you are healthy and full of life when you arrive. There is not another "you" in the whole wide world. Mommy also took what is called "Triple Test" to determine how you are doing in there. We are still unsure exactly how long your mother has been pregnant with you and we may have to get an ultrasound. – that means that we will see you on a screen. We're so proud of you. Keep growing!!!!

**Monday, October 20 – 16 weeks/5 days –** Your mother scheduled the appointment to have an ultrasound done to determine how long you have been growing. The appointment is this Friday at 1:30PM. Your mother is taking the rest of the day off but I will be going back to work. Your mother also sent me on my first food run thanks to your Uncle Andrew. Your uncle came by the house and mentioned something about "Church's Fried Chicken". Your mother thought that he had bought some to the house but was mistaken. However, by him mentioning chicken, your mother begged me to go out to get her some fried chicken. The nearest Church's was too far so we settled on Kentucky Fried Chicken. Half an hour later, she ate her chicken and I had leftover vegetable stew because I did not have enough money to buy myself some food.

**Friday, October 24 – 15 weeks/ 3 days** - We went to have the ultrasound done on Howell Mill Rd and we got to see you for the second time. The sonographer had to shake you to wake you up, but you look so cute on the screen. We saw your little head, fingers, toes, arms and legs wiggling. We even saw the left and right portions of your brain because your skin was so thin at this point in your development. The "not so good" news about the visit is that you are not as far as we thought. You registered as a fetus that is approximately fifteen weeks old. We thought you were at least 17 weeks. Because of this setback, your new due date is April 16, 1998, which is two weeks and two days after Uncle Alex's (my brother) birthday; two weeks after Grandma Beryl's (Mommy's mother) birthday; one day before Uncle Andrew's birthday; four days before Auntie Mel's (my sister). Mommy wants you to have your own birthday! We all know that you will come when you want to so take your time…. Just get here safely. We have a picture of you on the refrigerator and I kiss it every day.

**Friday, October 31 – 16 weeks/3 weeks** –Uncle Andrew and your cousins A.J. and Danny came by the house. Uncle Andrew was working on the Altima before we had to go to Kennesaw for a section leader rehearsal. Meanwhile, your mother and I left home to go to rehearsal in the Corolla. It was raining very hard. It took us an hour to get there, but because we did not know exactly where we were going, the weather made it difficult to see Auntie's Terri's (our choir director) house. Realizing that we must have passed the house because we could not see which road to turn on, we called the house to have someone come to the road to direct us.

As we were backtracking, we were going about 15 miles per hour in a pouring rain with the caution lights on. As I was driving, I spotted your Godfather Merle on my left signaling me to turn in there. So I signaled to turn left and started to do so. Suddenly I hear skidding tires on my side of the car. I looked and all I saw was the lights of a conversion van about to hit our car. The van rammed into the driver side of the car (my side), denting the door shut.  Mommy and I were alright but I was in shock for several minutes. I could not figure out how the man hit us. Obviously he was attempting to pass me on my left side as I was making the left into Auntie Terri's driveway. God is so awesome that He allowed us to suffer no ill effects from the wreck. After the police came and ticketed the other driver for illegal passing, we went inside and had rehearsal.  Mommy and I had something to be thankful for. All three of us were fine and God spared our health. Poor "Smokey" the car is banged up but she still runs. We will see about getting her fixed when we get the police report and file a claim against the other driver's insurance.

**Saturday, November 1 – 16 weeks/ 4 days** – Because we had such a long night, we decided to sleep in this morning, but you made Mommy pay for that!! Mommy eats every morning before she goes to work around 6:50a.m. Mommy did not get up until 9:30a.m. and when she did eat, she threw it up. Mommy was messed up the whole day. It was also very taxing on me because we had planned to share the cleaning chores around the house, but I was left to do it myself and take care of Mommy . I bet she won't lay up in the bed late again without eating.

**Tuesday, November 4 – 17 weeks** – I think this is the first time I have been able to put this development date in the journal. I can tell you are growing... is getting bigger by the day. Your mother still has not felt "flutters" yet, but I'm anticipating them any moment now. She has also been very good with her emotions until the day when she seemed very irritable all day. I try to calm her down any way I can when she gets like that because I want both of you to be happy. Mommy feels like she will be sixteen or seventeen weeks forever (due to the sonographer pushing back the due date). Take your time in there but don't take too much time. We want to see you healthy and happy.

**Tuesday, November 11 – 18 weeks** – We went to the midwife for a routine visit. Everything is fine... your heartbeat went to up 157 beats a minute!!!! That's excellent, baby!!! Keep pumping for Mommy and Daddy.

**Monday, November 17 – 18 weeks/6 days** – Mommy went to the midwife because she felt cramps in her side. Her blood pressure is slightly higher than normal. She didn't get much rest tonight because A.J. and Danny were at the house while Andrew was in the garage fixing the door on the Corolla. What would we do without Andrew? He has saved us hundreds of dollars on the car in the past two months. We must do something for him for all he has done. I know.... He can babysit when the baby comes? (just kidding!!!!)

**Friday, November 21 – 19 weeks/3 days** – Mommy thinks she felt a flutter today but she's not sure. You're right on schedule, Sweetness.

**Sunday, November 23 – 19 weeks/5 days** – Mommy definitely felt you move during the play "King of Glory" at the Atlanta Civic Center. Your Grandma Beryl was sitting with us when she felt you move. This is a very exciting time for us because this is the first time that we have "felt" your presence. Move about all you want but be easy on your mother. You will surely become stronger as you grow so don't kick her silly.

**Tuesday, November 25 – 20 weeks (5 months)** – WE ARE HALFWAY HOME!!!! This is considered the halfway point of your development in your mother's stomach. Mommy said that you were moving around when she got home and sat down. Mommy has grown to the point where it is harder to get up from a sitting and lying-down position. Each night Mommy comes in and brings me the lotion bottle so that I can put in on her after she showers. There is one thing that you should know about your mother she likes to be pampered and held just like you will like to be. So when you are born, make sure you give her lots of love and affection, and she promises to give it back. I have seen your mother go through a lot to carry you these five months and she still has a way to go. Always love your mother and you will be blessed!!

**Wednesday, November 26 – 20 weeks/1 day** – That is the first day of the second half of the pregnancy. By 6:50 this morning, your mother felt you moving about and began to talk directly to you. Before now, she would talk "about" you but never "to" you because she couldn't feel you yet. By now, I'm sure the in-depth conversations will begin. I can see the excitement in Mommy's face this week. It is no myth that pregnant women have a "glow" about them. When Mommy's happy, the baby is happy, and when the two of you are happy, Daddy's happy. Daddy likes to be happy. We are just one big happy family.

**Thursday, November 27 – 20 weeks 2 days** – We went to Dublin to see Grandma Dot on Thanksgiving Day and she had lots of food.  Mommy ate about three times today (I'm sure you got some of that, too!!!). We also saw your Great Grandma Glady's, cousins Chris, Erica, Shay, and Auntie Punchin (my aunt). Uncle Alex and the family came the next day. On the following Saturday, the Georgia Bulldogs beat Georgia Tech in a thriller 27-24 (in football). Who knows … you may want to attend our alma mater someday.

**Wednesday, December 3 – 21 weeks/1 day** –  Mommy says you're moving more frequently in the womb. Our next appointment is December 16. We basically have the system down now.  Mommy is getting more headaches and less nausea. I don't know if that is good or bad because I'm not experiencing either. This puts us in an awkward position because no mothers can make us fathers feel bad about not experiencing the pains of carrying a child. But everything they say is true…. There is no rebuttal. (Note: It's 22 days until Christmas … I'm sure this is a day you will learn to love!!!!)

**Saturday, December 6 – 21 weeks/ 4 days** – Tonight is the annual DMG Christmas party. Your mother is looking beautiful tonight in her burgundy velour dress. She looks so good that I had to pull out the tuxedo. The party was fun, but there were some lame gifts going around ... we played Dirty Santa... I'll explain it to you when you get older. We decided to stay at the hotel because it was late when the party finished. It was also very cold !!!!

**Tuesday, December 9 – 22 weeks** – Mommy threw up in my car today on our way to work (her car is in the shop for body work from the October 31 accident) Luckily she had a sandwich bag to do it in. I guess the sickness is not completely over. I don't feel good either .... I have a head cold that is draining my energy. All I can think about right now is a bed.

**Wednesday, December 10 – 22 weeks/ 1 day** – Mommy says you have been wiggling and moving all day. Are you excited about something, Baby? We can't wait until you're fully developed and ready to enter the world. A few weeks ago it was a few flutters .... now Mommy says that they feel like "thumps." I can only imagine what you will do to her in February or March!!! Grandma Dot says that I was an active baby too, when I was in her stomach. Maybe you're just like your father. For your mother's sake, I hope you are a little calmer.

**Saturday, December 13 – 22 weeks/ 4 days** – On our way to Uncle Jeff and Auntie Deion's house, Mommy almost "pee-ed" on herself when you kept rolling on her bladder. She would jump when you would turn because it would suddenly try to come out. It would have been a sight to see a puddle in the floor of the car if she could not hold it. Thank goodness that she did.

**Tuesday, December 16 – 23 weeks –** Your daddy had jury duty for the first time in his life today. Luckily I was dismissed because today is your monthly checkup. Mommy thinks she's big as a house but I have seen bigger at her stage of the pregnancy. At this visit your heartrate was 142 beats per minute and Mommy's stomach measured at approximately 25 centimeters (that 2 centimeters more than we expected) This may be an indication that you will arrive before April 16…. We hope so!!!). Mommy drank some coke for the first time in a while and she said that you were just wiggling all about in her stomach from the caffeine …. Bouncing from uterine wall to wall. Tell Mommy to give you notice before she takes a substance you're not used to. (It's nine days to Jesus' Birthday …. I can't wait!!!).

**Tuesday, December 23 – 24 weeks (6 months**) – Auntie Lorraine called your mother to tell her that your Mickey Mouse crib accessories were in K-Mart on Jimmy Carter Blvd, and boy, I tell you, your mother was so excited!!! So we rushed over there in the rain and spent a fortune …. But it was worth it. Now you have the comforter, bed sheets, pillow, musical mobile, and much, much more. By the way, Mommy is still throwing up… this time she said that something went down the wrong windpipe.

**Wednesday, December 24 (Christmas Eve) –** Mommy spent most of the morning in the bed with a headache but plans to get up later to go buy some items for the Christmas dinner @ Grandma Beryl's and Grandpa Dan's house on tomorrow. Grandma Dot will be in town later tonight … I'm sure much later.

**Thursday, December 25 (Christmas Day) –** This was a big Christmas for your Mommy. She got lots of maternity clothes and a camcorder. She was very surprised when she opened the box …. Daddy got a portable television, an electronic organizer, and some clothes. It was a good Christmas for me, too. You even got some baby stuff. Next year you will be here to celebrate it with us….. Much of your mother's family was in town to celebrate the holidays. We all had a good time!!!! I think Grandma Dot enjoyed herself as well. …. Auntie Shawn and Uncle Darren (our next-door neighbors) are giving us a stroller and swing for your arrival …. Isn't that great !!!! We have been so blessed and we haven't had a shower yet.

**Tuesday, December 30 (25 weeks)** – Mommy is showing pretty good now but I think she is not as big as women I have seen at this stage of the pregnancy. This year is almost over and shortly we will be saying "bye-bye" to 1997 and "hello" to 1998. Mommy says you were moving for much of the day on Monday. Keep growing …. It won't be long now.

**Sunday, January 4, 1998 (25 weeks/ 5 days)** This morning I felt you move for the first time. To your mother, it feels very distinct, but to me, it is slight.  tells me that you move a lot now…. I thank God that you are moving …. It lets me know that you are an active and lively baby and that's what your mother and I want. It's a brand new year and the Sanctuary Choir wore our new robes on the first Sunday of the year.  Mommy looked beautiful in her robe with her belly poking out. After church,  Mommy ate and took a long nap … She needed it because she seemed tired for the past week. One night last week, I could not go to sleep because your mother was snoring so loudly. It took me nearly two hours to finally fall asleep. I am not sure whether the excessive snoring is due to lack of sleep or that you are growing so much that you are restricting your mother's diaphragm to expand properly. Whatever the case I cannot sleep if I don't fall asleep first.  Mommy will stop in the middle of a conversation to ask you why you are moving so much. It's amazing to witness the bonding beginning to form between mother and child. What a privilege to bear a child.

**Tuesday, January 6, 1998 (26 weeks)** - Tonight is our annual choir awards night and mommy's last responsibility as Secretary of the choir. I hope I can find a video cassette tape that records for more than 30 minutes. Those tapes are just too short. I promise that I will get good camera shots of you tonight, "cinnamon drop." You know Daddy love that baby.

**Thursday, January 8, 1996 (26 weeks / 2 days)** – Poor Mommy !!! Her entire body aches so bad she literally cried herself to sleep tonight. I tried to massage her back and shoulders, but I do not know if that did any good. She got out of bed slowly the next morning. I hope you know what you are putting your mother through because if you forget I will remind you.

**Friday, January 9, 1998 (26 weeks - 3 days)** Mommy called me to tell me that a co-worker conducted the pencil test on her and said that the baby will be a girl because the pencil went in a circle around her wrist. She also told me that she saw her stomach move for the first time. I can't wait to see that!!!! Remember that car accident in October? We just got in contact with a liability representative after over a month. She never returns our calls and we had some very important information to share with her. Mommy scared her half to death by asking to speak with her supervisor. After she told us all these lies about why she didn't get in touch with us for over a month, we decided to write a letter to her supervisor to state our dissatisfaction regarding the quality of service she provided. You will understand that the Smith's don't take junk off of anyone when we are paying for a service (especially your mother... I was not always like this).  Mommy said that when I came in the door and spoke one day, you started wiggling in her stomach. Do you know Daddy's voice now? See, Daddy and Mommy want you to be proud of us as we are proud of you. This is the first time for all of us and we want it to be special. You will be our first child. No one can take that away from you. When you are all grown up, we want you to be able to say, " I have the best parents a child could ever have."

**Saturday, January 17, 1998 (27 weeks 4 days)** Today we had a surprise baby shower for Uncle Dudley and Auntie Claire (your God parents) and your God brother (well, your mother and I believe that it's a boy while everyone else believes it's a girl). Uncle Dudley has not come up with the name if it's a boy so we will see when the baby comes. If it's a girl your God sister's name will be Grace Noble White. I say the baby will come on January 29th. Your mother says February 3rd; Uncle Dudley says January 24th. I don't know what Auntie Claire thinks. I guess she will just be happy just to deliver soon.  Mommy experienced what she believes to be hiccups. She also feels pain in her right hip. We pray that she will not have to go on bed rest before term. You are sitting so low in Mommy's tummy that she is experiencing discomfort in her hips. At every opportunity I try to get her off her feet to rest and elevate her legs. Her hands and feet are swelling more now too. Mommy was poking you while lying on the sofa and she said you kicked her. I guess you didn't want to be bothered.

**Monday, January 19, 1998 (27 weeks 6 days)** Today we celebrate Dr. Martin Luther King Jr's birthday (even though the actual date is January 15th) and your mother and I spent the day doing productive stuff. After we went to Shoney's with Auntie Lorraine for breakfast and drop by MLS to pick up my lock box key, your mother and I went to Toys R Us to complete a baby register... that's right we were registering to get goodies for you, like diapers, onesies, baby bath set, bassinet and lots more. In the March 1st journal entry, I'll tell you all the things you got from all the people who love you. Your mother's agility is becoming more limited as the pregnancy progresses. Before now she would try to do everything by herself. Now I believe she realizes that she needs help to get in and out of the car or the bed. She also is finding it difficult to find clothes to wear to church. I told her she can start wearing pant outfits.  Mommy says that the light flutters are over, they have now become strong kicks.

**Tuesday, January 20, 1998 (28 weeks)**  Mommy had her monthly appointment today and her blood pressure was slightly high. She thinks it's diet-related (She had a processed turkey sandwich for breakfast). I told her that she must rest more when she gets home from work. When she elevates her feet the swelling tends to go down in her feet.

**Saturday, January 24, 1998 ( 28 weeks 4 days)** Today is the day Uncle Dudley predicted that their baby would arrive. Well... Auntie Claire has not felt anything and may not for a while. Mommy said you woke her up this morning. You have been so active lately. Our next appointment with the midwife is February 2nd at 4 p.m. Our regular midwife did not meet with us on our last visit and I did not like the one that conducted our exam. I hope Catherine will be there next week. (note: Unleaded gas is 84 cents/ gallon today. Can you believe that?)

**Sunday, January 25, 1998 (28 weeks 5 days)** The Denver Broncos upset the favored Green Bay Packers 31-24 in Super Bowl XXXII. Terrell Davis (who attended the University of Georgia - your parents alma mater) won Most Valuable Player honors scoring a record-setting three touchdowns. Also in the news, President Clinton is accused for having "improper relations" with a female intern working in the White House. I'll explain "improper relations" to you when you are old enough to understand.

**Wednesday, January 28, 1998 (29 weeks 1 day)** Poor Mommy had another accident this morning. Of course, she was totally hysterical when she called me on the phone at 8:30 a.m. She hit another car from behind while trying to beat a yellow light. The problem was the driver decided to stop abruptly causing your mother to ram into him. And if that wasn't enough... The guy worked at an auto body repair shop and had his people estimate the cost at $2,500. By the looks of the damage to our car, the charges could not possibly be that much. I'm just happy that both of you are alright. Mommy went to the doctor and they confirmed that you were just fine. This is the second wreck in 3 months. We don't want anything to happen to you or us.

**Saturday, January 31, 1998 (29 weeks/4 days)** Auntie Lorraine just moved into her house on Thursday and Mommy and I helped her with the move-in. We have been very busy and Mommy is very tired. We will probably sing only one service tomorrow.

**Monday, February 2, 1998 (29 weeks/6 days)** This , by far, was the worst doctor appointment that we have had. First of all, your mother and I waited in the lobby for forty minutes to see the mid-wife, only to find out that she was too busy with other patients and so another midwife had to see us. Then the "wrong midwife" began calling your mother, "Brenda Smith," which was obviously another patient at the clinic. Then she began to ask crazy questions about things that Mommy was not even experiencing. It was a very bad visit and Daddy was highly upset. We didn't find out your heartrate because this woman could not use the monitor properly. From now on, we will be visiting the clinic every two weeks until the $36^{th}$ week: then it increases to once a week. Time has been flying lately but we do not want to rush you. We need you to stay in Mommy's stomach until you can safely live comfortably outside. So take your time.

**Saturday, February 7, 1998 (30 weeks 4 days)** Daddy painted the baby's new bedroom today. If you forgot, the theme is Disney characters and the primary colors are red, yellow, and blue. It is so pretty. We will try to assemble the baby crib tomorrow. Daddy is very tired. I've done everything from the baby room to lawn work to house cleaning to cooking. God bless those single mothers and fathers who have no help.

**Wednesday, February 11, 1998 (31 weeks 1 day)** - It's Daddy's 29th birthday and I thank God that I am able to see another year go by. Some people have already called to wish me a happy birthday, and I'm sure a few more will call. Mommy just love birthdays as if they were all hers. I will get my present later today... I don't know what it is but I'm sure it is something I have wanted or needed for quite some time. Auntie Claire and Uncle Dudley still haven't delivered your god brother or sister. If it does not arrive by the 19th, the doctor will induce Auntie Claire's labor so that she can have the baby. Uncle Dudley says the baby will probably be at 8 pounds. That's a big boy! I wonder if you will be that big?

**Thursday, February 12, 1998 (31 weeks/ 2 days)** Just as we suspected..... Your god brother was born at 8:38 a.m. at Northside Hospital (that's where you'll be born). His name is Harrison Isaiah White and he weighed 7 lb. and 3 oz. Your mother and I went to visit Uncle Dudley, Auntie Claire, and Isaiah and the hospital. They were doing just fine and can't wait to see you. I'm sure you will see the video tape of our visit when you get older.

**Wednesday, February 18, 1998 (32 weeks 1 day)** - This was the first appointment that I did not attend and from what your mother said I did not miss anything. She told me you were doing fine and your heartbeat your heart rate is at 144 beats a minute. Mommy seems to have grown considerably in the past few weeks.... We have considered the possibility of your arrival coming in late March or early April. You should be proud of your mother. She gets up every morning to go to work and most days I know she would rather stay in the bed. She lately has had some congestion, but the midwife says it's normal. Everything is normal to them.

**Saturday, February 21, 1998 (32 weeks 4 days)** - Grandma Dot's House was "The Infirmary" this weekend. We had planned to visit your grandmother, but by Thursday, I was coming down with what eventually turned out to be the flu. Two hours I drove to Dublin Friday evening, sniffling and sneezing. I think I gave it to your mother on the way down there, because she began to feel bad the next day. I feel bad about it because Mommy cannot take medication like I can, and it may take longer to fight it off. Grandma Dot gave me some "rabbit tobacco and "moss juice" and it cleared it up by late Sunday. Being pregnant is bad enough for your mother; now we have to fight the flu. Will it ever end?

**Sunday, February 22, 1998 (32 weeks 5 days)** - Mommy and I returned from Dublin to go to a surprise birthday party for Uncle Chris (that's my hometown best friend). He turned 29 just like me. Later that night, I watched you kick your mother half to death. You have been a very active baby lately. Mommy believes she is experiencing Braxton-Hicks contractions now. Today is also the 10th anniversary of the passing of your Grandpa Alex. We visited the cemetery before we left Dublin. IN THE NEWS::There was a threat that the United States will go to war against the country of Iraq, but a peaceful agreement has been reached. I don't expect you to understand now.... prophecies are being fulfilled.

**Sunday, March 1, 1998 (33 weeks 5 days)** - Today was a big day for you. Today we had our first baby shower at Auntie Lorraine's house and it was a BIGGGGGGGG one. Over 60 people showed up to give you presents for your expected arrival. God has truly blessed us with so much stuff (even before the shower). Most of it was given to us for free.... And we count it a blessing to have such a great family and friends who feel led to give us stuff out of the goodness of their heart. There isn't too much left that we need for you. Mommy is making a "wish list" for those people who did not attend the shower, but still want to give us something. Mommy's co-workers are also throwing you a shower at her job on March 16th. Auntie Shawn (our next door neighbor) gave us a deluxe stroller and swing yesterday.

**Tuesday, March 3, 1998 (34 week)** - We're coming down the stretch run. Mommy had a rough day at work on Monday and had a big cry that night. She says those make her feel better, but I don't like to see her cry. This pregnancy has had some ups and downs and it has really taken its toll on your mother. Your mother is a strong woman and it's showing during these times. We are treading into uncharted territory now so this experience is new for all of us... But it is very exciting and the fun has just begun. Uncle Brent called tonight... It was his 30th birthday yesterday. He is convinced that you are a boy. We have a bet if you're a girl, he will have to buy a pretty baby outfit. If you are a boy, we will take him to Rafferty's Restaurant in Athens.

**Thursday, March 5, 1998 (34 weeks / 2 days)** - I went with Mommy to her doctor's appointment to get a routine check on you. Your heart rate is at 151 beats/minute, which is still consistent with our theory that you could possibly be a girl. Trying to guess the sex has been fun but I don't know if we will ever do it again (that is, wait until delivery to find out the sex of the child). It is killing us not to know your sex, but I admit it is interesting to hear everyone's hunches about you. Mommy says you have been an active all day long. I watched you as you stretched, kicked, and poked at your mother's stomach. Getting a little cramped in there? Your Daddy doesn't like to be in confined places either, but it is a necessity of life that we all have to experience. Believe me that you will not remember this when you are on the outside. After our next clinic visit, we will be asked to come in once a week. It won't be long now.

**Friday, March 6, 1990 (34 weeks 3 days)** - Your mother woke up this morning and heard a "pop" in her midsection. She asks a nurse at her job and she told her it is probably her pelvis joint separating to accommodate you for delivery. You will be here before we know it. I still can't believe there will one day be a little face looking up at me and calling me Daddy. It hasn't sunk in yet but I'm sure reality will set in shortly.

**Sunday, March 8, 1998 (34 weeks / 5 days)** – It was a very wet and rainy day today..... Mommy and I went to an Asian restaurant for the first time since we have been married. The food was okay but I don't believe that we will be going there anytime soon. The store rating was 84 (Mommy doesn't like to go anywhere under 90). We watched the movie "Contact" later this evening with Jodie Foster and Matthew McConnerhay (I know this is misspelled) and it was not that good..... A tragedy happened tonight in Carrollton where a mother lost her 20 month-old child in a flooded creek. The maternal instinct in your mother must have really kicked in because she cried just by hearing the news. We said a prayer for that family and hope that everything turns out all right. News like this helps one to understand that there are indeed joys and fears in raising a child. We pray that the joys outweigh the fears with you.

**Thursday, March 12, 1998 (35 weeks - 2 days)** - Mommy is experiencing Braxton Hicks contractions and you will not stop. You must like the right side of mommy's stomach because you are heavily lopsided on that side. Is it getting cramped in there, sugar? It won't be long before you are due. Just wait until we have our child birthing classes. Then your mother and I will have some confidence before you decide to arrive.

**Saturday, March 14, 1998 (35 weeks 4 days)** We have the first session of the child birthing class today. Your mother was in there answering all the questions like she knew it all. I'm sure the other couples in the classes we're thinking," if she knows all the answers, then why did she attend this class?" The breathing techniques we're helpful to me because I had to be your mother's coach through the birthing process. I feel a little better now because all I have to do is make sure that Mommy breathes through her contractions. I can do that..... I think.

**Sunday, March 15, 1998 (35 weeks 5 days)** 7:30 a.m. - Mommy woke to "strong Braxton Hicks contractions". Of course I was asleep at this time. Mommy woke me at 8:15 a.m. Mommy slept in the Alpha room last night because she could not go to sleep with my snoring (I guess I beat her to the punch this time).

**8:30 a.m**. - Mommy tried to walk the contractions away. We paced in the kitchen to the dining room and back around. I followed her still half asleep praying that the contractions will go away. She said that they were the worst she felt so far.

**9:15 a.m.** - I cooked Mommy a waffle for breakfast. She ate it and fell asleep on the loveseat in the family room. I went upstairs to do something (I forgot what I went upstairs for but I stayed there for quite a while).

**10:25 a.m.** - I decided that I would go to the grocery store since Mommy didn't feel too well. I came downstairs to put on my shoes when suddenly Mommy woke up shouting, "Did you hear that"? I answered, "What?" "That pop..... did I "pee" on myself or did my water break? I checked her gown and indeed she was wet. Mommy went to the bathroom and the water continue to flow. After we overcame the initial shock we concluded that her water had broken. But so soon? We still have two to four weeks so we thought. We didn't even get to finish our child birthing class that resumed at 2 p.m. today. Mommy was shaking like a leaf for anticipation of what would occur shortly. I, on the other hand, was fairly calm (to my surprise) I had the emergency number to the clinic and told them all that had happened. They told us to go to the hospital, so we put on our clothes, gathered our items and headed for Northside Hospital. At this time the contractions had subsided. We didn't know what this meant but it did make for an easy ride to the hospital.

**11:45 a.m.** - Mommy checked into the Labor and Delivery room at Northside Hospital. At this time Mommy was experiencing irregular contractions. The midwife (Ellen Martin) confirmed that the water had broken but Mommy was not in active labor yet. Ellen said that Mommy was 80% effaced and only a fingertip dilated. They were going to monitor her to see if she goes into active labor soon..... If not then she would be moved to a private room until active labor begins. Mommy was fine at this time. Auntie Lorraine met us at the hospital when we were checking in. Grandma Beryl and Grandpa Dan came later after evening service.

**5:15 p.m**. - Mommy was still experiencing regular contractions and the nursing staff decided to transfer us to a private room (Room 339) until the contractions became more consistent. Mommy received her first meal since breakfast this morning. She talked the nurse (her name was Beth) into giving her a double portion. Beth was very nice. After we moved upstairs Auntie Lorraine left to go home.

**10:30 p.m.** - The contractions have began occurring more frequently and stronger. She had two contractions in the six o'clock hour; three in each of the next two hours; and four in the nine o'clock hour. I'm trying to be the good coach and help Mommy stay on top of those contractions.

**11:40 p.m.** - Active labor begins. I begin timing them and they were consistently five minutes apart. Mommy is doing excellent with her breathing. Our nurse on the third floor (her name is Marie) was very comforting and nice. These contractions were taking more energy than those earlier.

**Monday, March 16, 1998 (35 week/6 days) 1:45 a.m.** - Daddy put in his contacts because I knew that they were going to move us back to Labor and Delivery soon. Mommy was having to work harder to stay on top of the contractions with her breathing but she was doing great. I could see that the contractions were tiring her out. The nurse begin to prepare to move us downstairs.

**2:15 a.m.** - The pains were becoming close to unbearable for Mommy. When Ellen checked Mommy to see how far along she had come, Mommy was in so much pain I could not bear to take you. She had only dilated 2 to 3 cm. I was praying that they would decide to give her medication for the contractions so she may get some comfort. Auntie Lorraine and Grandma Beryl had arrived at the hospital by this time.

**3 a.m.** - The doctor came by to give Mommy a shot in her back to relieve the pain. Believe me…. This pain medicine really works. Shortly afterwards, Mommy fell asleep but the contractions on the monitor were strong and hard. If Mommy had not received the medication, she would have been climbing the walls by now. Thank God for effective medication. I can hardly stay awake during the waiting because I was running on 45 minutes of sleep in the past 20 hours.

**7:30 a.m.** - Although the pain from the contractions were surprised, Mommy still felt the pressure in the lower abdomen, Ellen checked Mommy and she had effaced 100 percent and was nearly nine centimeters dilated. The good news gave Mommy a jolt of energy to make it down the home stretch. Your birth was on the horizon. A cup of coffee gave me some energy earlier but now the excitement of your arrival was all I needed to bring me through.

**8:46 a.m.** - After nearly 36 weeks of anticipation, my little girl Kennedi Alexander Smith was born. You weighed only 4 pounds and 8 ounces and measured 18 1/2 in long. You should have seen your mother's face when they place you on her stomach only seconds after your birth. If you could put the love that radiated from her face in a bottle, it would be worth a fortune. I have seen you go from a dot on the screen to a tiny person in our arms. Your mother and I love you, Kennedi, and we promise to do everything we can to provide you with the best that we can offer. We pray that God will forever keep his Loving Hands on you and protect you at all times. You have family and friends that love you and are glad to see you come to us in good health. May God bless you on this journey we call "Life".

### You will always be "Our Firstborn Child."

# Mommy

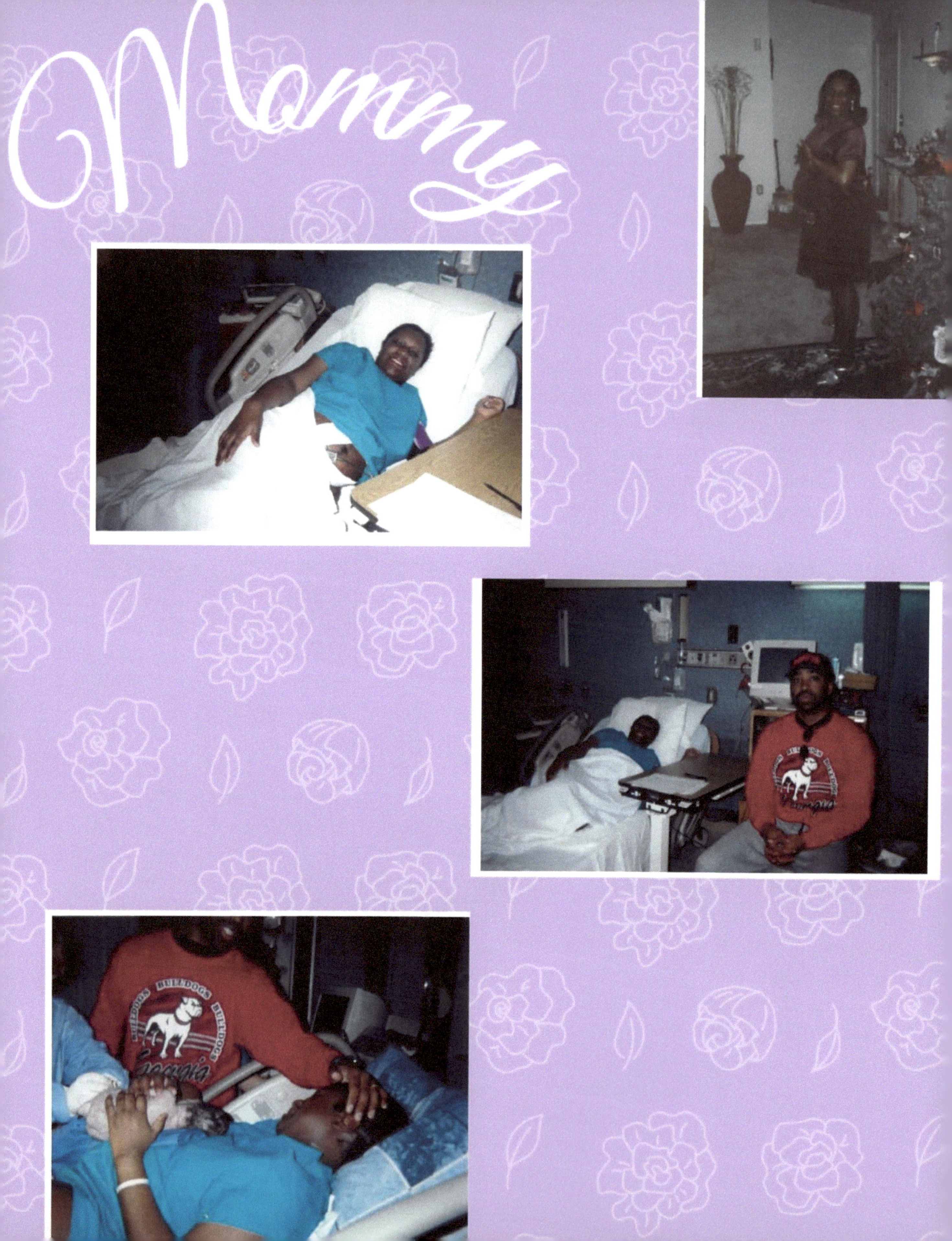

Kennedi

"Help him grow to become a healthy and strong man in your image. Help us as parents to guide him in the right direction and give him guidance to start his life." I feel like this prayer to God was answered. I am here now writing a Prologue for the man that has raised me for the last 17 years. Before I was even born having to deal with moving to another home and taking care of a 4-year-old child all while preparing for another child is a daunting task that I can't even imagine taking on myself. All while my mother was uncertain about her employment status after the pregnancy. This highlights the strength it took to go through this and this same strength my father prayed to god to give me. However, God did not just bless me with this strength, this strength was taught to me through my parents. This prayer was answered through their own will. Now I get to look back at how things were folding out before I came into the world. This Journal revealed things that I did not know at first including the crazy hairstyles my mother wore that garnered the attention of her co-workers. I wish I could go back in time to see what she wore to just have a laugh at what my mother was doing during her stages with me.

Love, Myles

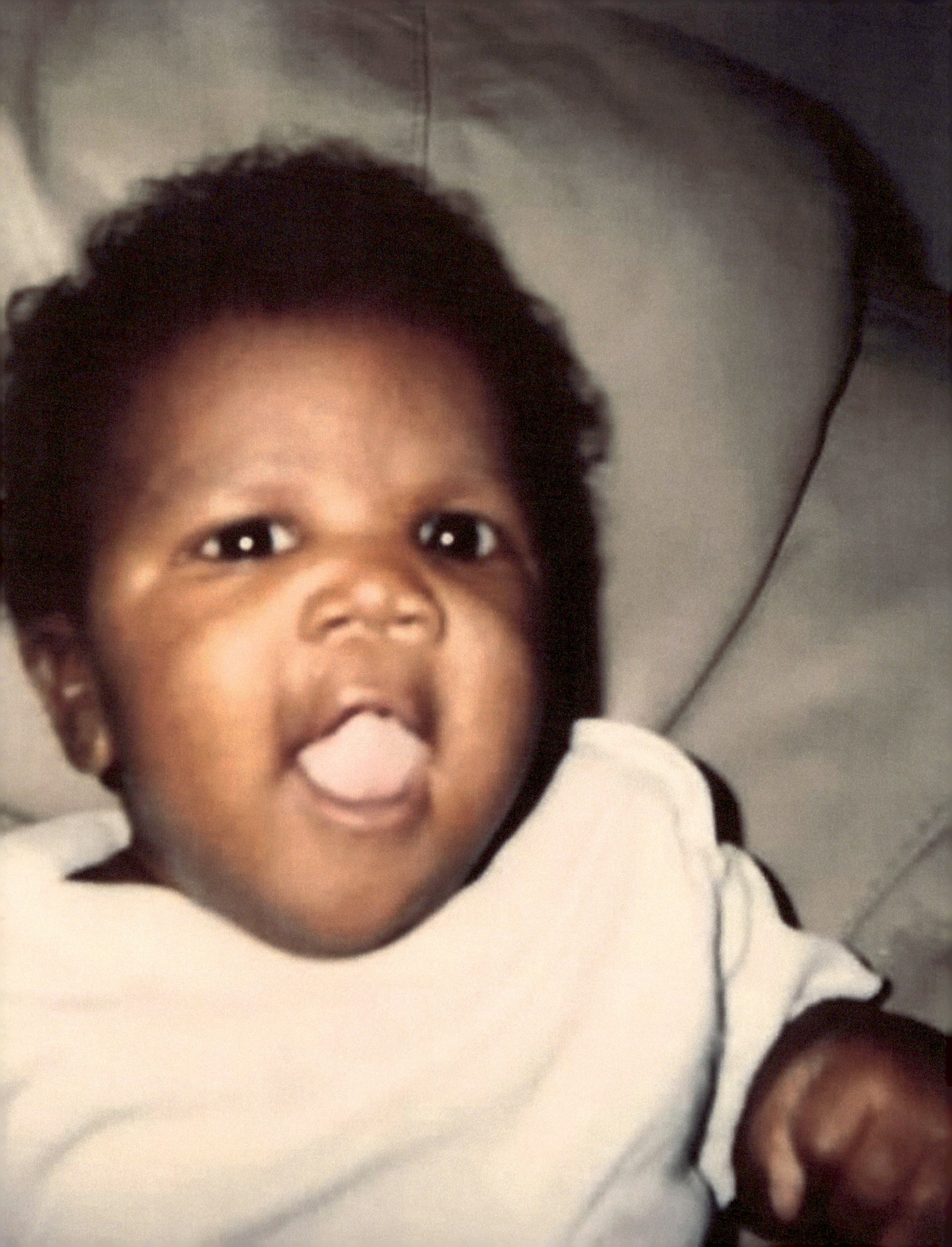

# Daddy's Journal II

**Thursday, June 20, 2002** I woke up to....."I just can't believe it.. I am pregnant!" Wow, we are having another child. After five years, we are heading down this road again. Since it is so early in the pregnancy Mommy, you and I are the only ones who know. I probably won't tell people until sometime in August. Just hang tight and don't give your Mommy too much trouble.

**Sunday, July 14, 2002** Today was a very scary day for Daddy. Mommy was taking a nap on the couch in the living room when I reached into the trash can to pull out a glass pitcher that had broken. When I grabbed the picture by its shaft.....CRACK. I stood in the kitchen in shock praying that I didn't cut myself but I got the answer to that prayer when blood began seeping through the creases of the hand. Now my prayer was that I had all ten fingers still intact. After five seconds and paralyzed in shock, I rushed to the downstairs bathroom with a blood trail to follow. I washed the cut and wrapped it with a towel not knowing the degree of the damage. Ms. Pam (your sister Kennedi's daycare provider and our friend) hurried to pick up Kennedi while Mommy took me to the emergency room. I was fortunate that I only cut my middle finger on my left hand. The bad news is that I had to receive seven stitches. It really hurts. I'll show you the war wound when you get older.

**Tuesday, July 16, 2002** I'm tired of being secretive about this pregnancy. We broke down and told Uncle Dudley and Auntie Claire (who are also pregnant with their 3rd child) but that's it. I can't wait to tell Kennedi. She is going to love on you like nobody's business. Mommy is experiencing more fatigue and nausea. I burned some popcorn tonight.... That's a mistake because Mommy hates the smell of burnt popcorn. Daddy has been working like a dog at work. I'm scheduled to go on a day trip to Austin, Texas next week. It's only for a day.

**Thursday, July 25, 2002 (9 weeks / 5 days)** Mommy has been experiencing lots of fatigue with you. This is much different from the nausea she had with Kennedi. She is taking naps during her lunch break to take the edge off at work. People are now wondering whether she is pregnant. Her clothes are looking rather tight these days.

**Saturday, July 27, 2002 (10 weeks)** The family went to see Grandma Dot and she seemed to know right away that Mommy was pregnant with you. We decided to tell grandma because we were finding it hard to hide the pregnancy. Mommy is getting bigger by the day. We also went to the church campground that I once attended as a child. It was fun to see the old friends and sites. Uncle Alex preached and did a great job. Grandma Dot is so proud of him because she feels that he has grown so much as a minister.

**Tuesday, July 30, 2002 (10 weeks / 3 days)** Today is a baby checkup day and just as I did with Kennedi I plan to attend all of Mommy's monthly checkups with you. This was an especially exciting appointment because we got to see how you have developed thus far. We saw your head and arms beginning to form. We even watched your little heart pulsating through a tenuous layer of skin...WOW. The doctor (Dr. Sermon)...wiggled Mommy's tummy to make you move and boy did you move.  Mommy was grinning so hard because she actually got to see you move for the first time. Your due date is February 20, 2003 (nine days after my birthday) Mommy also found out that Auntie Joanna and Uncle Stephen are expecting as well. Looks like the maternity ward in the hospital will be busy around February/March. Sometimes I wonder whether I have lost my paternal skills in infant care. I'm sure they will come back but it is somewhat scary. I want you to have the same love and attention as we give Kennedi. That will be a sacrifice because one child demands so much attention, yet alone two. Mommy drove the mock commute to the new office today. Let's just say that her days at the Corban Group are numbered. I don't know how long she will last but one day of bouting nausea and traffic may set her off. I believe her resignation letter is already written in her mind. All in all, today has been a good day.

**Sunday, August 4, 2002 (11 weeks/1 day)** Your mother wanted Jamaican food today and we went to great lengths to find it – – let's try an hour of driving around. It was after 6 p.m. and most of the Jamaican stores were closed. We finally stopped at Cool Running on Memorial Drive. We asked Uncle Andrew to join us.

Auntie Angie (God-mother) gave Mommy lots of maternal clothes to wear. She needs them because Mommy is about to burst out of her clothes. It took her twenty minutes in the morning to find something in the closet to fit.

Mommy got a great blessing when her manager (Cliff) allowed her to leave work at 4 p.m. instead of 4:30 p.m. That allows her to pick up Kennedi in time from daycare. I think it will also help her feel better about going to work each day. God has poured out his favor on Mommy and is storing up massive treasures for her in Heaven. Daddy is proud to call Mommy his wife and you'll be proud to call her "Mommy." You can ask Kennedi.

**Sunday, August 11, 2002 (12 weeks /1 day)** Guess what? I cut my finger... Again. Where? In the garbage can.... Again. I'm so embarrassed. What is up with pregnancies and cut hands? This time it happened on my right wrist when I was pushing the trash in the garbage can. There was a sharp object protruding from the bag that raked across my wrist. I didn't think anything of it and thought it was a minor scrape (it was dim in the garage). When I went back into the house I felt something running down my arm. It was blood. Not again. Mommy was upstairs taking a shower. I was so embarrassed because we have this running joke that I will always cut my hands when Mommy is pregnant. I hurried upstairs to get a bandage but I could not stop the bleeding. It was almost bedtime so I thought for sure that she would find out what happened. I finally got the bleeding to stop so I could place the bandage on it. I kept my arm turned to my body for the rest of the night so that mommy could not see it. At one point she looked at me as if something was wrong but I told her that I was fine. Kennedi saw the bandage and asked me why I had one on. I thought she would surely tell Mommy that Daddy had another band-aid on. She didn't (Thank God). The things we do to save face.

**Monday, August 12, 2002 (12 weeks /2 days)** It was your sister's first day at Pre-k. Actually she still goes to Ms. Pam's Learning Center but Pam decided to start pre-k this year. That saved us the hassle of finding a school for Kennedi this year. Mommy wants to move to another school district before Kennedi goes to kindergarten. I'm sure God will make a way.

About me? Daddy is praying about whether he should post for the team lead at work. My manager (Ms. Lisa) left the position to take a job at McDonald's group. I know it will be more money but for some reason my heart is not in it to apply. I'm not sure whether I'm nervous about the added responsibility or God is trying to tell me that it is not my time. I'm trusting in God for this one. I just hope that I'm obedient no matter what He says.

Getting back to your mother... Just to let you know how strange your mother has been acting lately. Before she was pregnant with you, Mommy would never eat anything spicy. Now she has this liking for chicken with hot sauce. These cravings are a new twist to the pregnancy. Mommy had only one craving while carrying Kennedi and that was for Kentucky Fried Chicken. The 1st trimester is almost over. Thank God that all is well thus far.

**Saturday, August 17, 2002 (13 weeks - beginning of 2nd trimester)** Auntie Tammy (your Godmother) got married today and it was a beautiful ceremony and reception. Mommy served as a matron of honor and was very pretty too. She still feels sick every now and then but not as bad as expected. As you will learn, Daddy is a big baseball fan. Well, the players have set August 30th as a strike date and they cannot come to terms with the owners on a new labor agreement. The union has gone on a strike eight times before in the last 30 years and if it happens this time I may be done with it. Millionaires are fighting over more millions. It's ridiculous. Bring on football.

**August 18, 2002 (13 weeks/1 day)** It's Grandpa Dan's (Mommy's father), 70th birthday and the kids gave him a surprise birthday party with about 20 of his closest friends. We have food left over to eat throughout the week. Mommy was very tired today and went to bed early. All she's doing is sleeping and eating but it doesn't seem that she is gaining much weight yet.

**Monday, August 19, 2002 (13 weeks/2 days)** Mommy felt very sick today and decided to come home early from work. The doctor prescribed a suppository for nausea. Not only does it suppress nausea but it also causes drowsiness - like your mother needs anything to help her sleep. Mommy took one suppository and was asleep by 8:45 p.m. She was snoring, grunting, and talking in her sleep all night. It was so loud at one point that I almost left the room to sleep in the computer room. I eventually fell asleep over the snoring rendition given by Mommy and Kennedi in unison.

**Thursday, August 22, 2002 (13 weeks 5 days)** We just finished the leftovers from Grandpa Dan's birthday party and man were they good!!!!!! Mommy said that you seemed very pleased after every meal. Mommy has been acting very strange lately, almost like she is trying to start little arguments. Daddy has come a long way since your mother and I were married nearly seven years ago. And our early years I would get "sucked into" those arguments and later realize that I just ranted and raved over silly stuff. Now I just brush it off and live to see another day. Mommy wouldn't admit this but I see a little hormonal imbalance in this pregnancy. Her fuse is shorter than normal. Are you easily irritated?

Mommy likes the name Paxston for a girl. I don't know if I like it yet. Maybe it will grow on me. I need to hear it with a strong middle name.

**Friday, August 30, 2002 (14 weeks 6 days)** Mommy, Daddy, and Kennedi left for Destin, Florida for a long holiday weekend. Monday is also Mommy and Daddy's 7th wedding anniversary. The ride took five and a half hours and we were tired of being in the car that long. We met Auntie Claire and Uncle Dudley down there. I'm sure we all will have a blast on the beach.

**Monday, September 2, 2002 (15 weeks / 2 days)** I would be remiss if I did not wish my wife a very Happy Anniversary ( Mommy, I know before you would be reading this at some point so I thought it would be in my best interest to extend this wish). I haven't noticed a huge change in Mommy in the past few weeks. She is still experiencing mild headaches and some nausea. Her main ailment is her hips become disjointed at times. She says that you are feeling increasingly heavy in her pelvic area. If my memory serves me correctly this did not start happening with Kennedi until the seventh or eight month. Boy, we may be in for an eventful journey with you.

**Wednesday, September 4, 2002 (15 weeks 4 days)** We are back home now from vacation and Mommy and I decided to casually go out to view new homes. Well, we stopped at one subdivision called Embassy walk in Gwinnett County. The subdivision is about 5 minutes from Uncle Dudley and Auntie Claire's house and I believe Mommy has fallen in love in this floor plan called the Sussex. I must admit that I like it too. It has five bedrooms and two-and-a-half baths with a basement option. It's in the school district that Mommy wants Kennedi to attend. We spoke to the agent on site and said that if we agree to a contract today it would be about six months to build and be ready for occupancy. That's about the same time that you are due to be born, which would be a tremendous strain on your mother and me. We don't know how your mother will be faring in a couple of months from now and I would not want to stress her by asking her to help with getting our current home ready for sale. This is a life lesson: God may place us in positions which may make us feel somewhat uncomfortable but at the same time pushing us to move forward by faith. Mommy's employment status after you are born is very much uncertain. She doesn't know whether she will return to the Corban group. My thought is that she would return...... If she doesn't it would be reluctantly. If Mommy decides not to go back, I do not know how we can afford a larger mortgage. Only God knows. He will make a way.

**Tuesday, September 10, 2002 (16 weeks 3 days)** I had to leave early to pick up mommy from work because she was experiencing dizzy spells. It took nearly an hour to get there from Coke and an hour to get from her job home. The doctor says that it may be due to hormonal fluctuations and low blood sugar. Mommy has some orange juice and took a nap when we got home. She felt much better later this evening. Mommy and Daddy have still been discussing the Sussex. The question is not are we moving, it's when we are moving. My heart is telling me to schedule the move after you are born (April or May). We still have the issue of when do we put our house up for sale and who can we stay with while the house is being built? Maybe it's a re - sale that we should be looking for? I don't know.

**Thursday, September 12, 2002 (16 weeks 5 days)** Your mother just called me at work to tell me that she is craving a tomato w/ mayo on a bagel. What's strange about this is she doesn't even like tomatoes. It appears that the craving is so strong that she has asked one of her co-workers (Tom Williams) to go to the grocery store to buy "one" tomato. WOW!!!!! Mommy has it bad. You should hear her on the phone practically salivating on the receiver talking about how good this tomato bagel will be. I hope it is good for her sake. Stay tuned ...... I'm positive that this entry is not over.
For now, if you are a boy it will be *Myles Arrington Smith*; if a girl *Chandler Danielle Smith*

Back to the bagel....... Mommy called me back to let me know that the bagel was so good that she is wondering why she hasn't had it before. Could it be because..... SHE HATES TOMATOES. Sometimes I feel that I do not even know your mother anymore. She thinks I would like it because she knows that I like tomatoes. Believe me when I say ..... There is NO ONE like your dear mother.

**Saturday, September 14, 2002 (17 weeks)** Mommy and Daddy dropped Kennedi off at Auntie Lorraine's house and went back to Embassy Walk subdivision. David (the on-site agent) showed us a finished Savannah floorplan and we loved it. Mommy was especially impressed with the details in the home. That floorplan with a basement would look great on Lot #26 (I'm claiming that !!!!) Mommy threw up at the traffic light on the corner of Five Forks Trickum and Hall. It was all in the street and the people in the cars next to us were all grossed out. It was embarrassing but funny to see the expression of their faces when Mommy threw up her breakfast.

**Saturday, September 21, 2002 (18 weeks)** We signed a contract to buy the Lot #26 in Embassy Walk. I'm sick just thinking about how I just signed my whole life away to this house, but I know it's going to be beautiful when it finally goes up. The projected closing date is March 31, 2003 which means that you should be here by the time we move in. So much is changing so fast ..... Now we must think about our current home..... That is selling it fast!!! The faster we are out of this house the better we will be moving into the new one. We are all praying for a smooth transition. Your job is to  grow and hang tight. You still have a while to go.

**Monday, September 30, 2002 (what I thought was 19 weeks/2 days)** The moment of truth has arrived ...... we just found that you are........ A BOY!!!!!!!!! We are so excited! All I could say in the doctor's office was "Yes! Yes!". Mommy was smiling from ear to ear because she and I know that this is it!! Our family is complete. We have one girl and now you. Up to this moment I had this peace in my soul that you were a boy but could not totally convince myself that was the case. God has confirmed that peace and now there is a huge relief for the manifestation. I prayed earnestly for a son and now I feel that my desire was God's will for this family. You can be proud to know that your mother and I take our parenthood seriously and we vow to love and cherish you just like we do your big sister now. The whole reason for keeping such a journal is to let you know that how much we love you and we owe you the best that life can offer.

The nurse gave us more good news that you are further along than expected. We thought that you were slightly over 19 weeks but the nurse measured your head and limbs and calculated that you are closer to 20 weeks. That's just like giving Mommy a birthday present because that means cutting a week off the due date. After we called family and friends, Mommy and I went home and let it all soak in.. Mommy broke down with tears of joy praising God that you are healthy. I thought I would be the one crying my heart out but I kept walking around the house with that "That's my boy!!!!!" feeling in my soul. Now I know how it felt when my dad found out I had been accepted to attend the University of Georgia. It is so good to know that I can call you "son". By the way, don't get used to the name I wrote in an earlier entry .... That will probably change.

**Monday, October 7, 2002 (21 weeks/1 day)** Daddy is back from a golf trip to Destin and we are days away from placing the "For Sale" sign in the front yard. I'm so tired but I will be relieved when we finally put the house on the market, Mommy said that you are kicking and moving all around. Time seems to be going fast. Mommy may have a different opinion on that.

**Wednesday, October 9, 2002 (21 weeks/3 days)** Mommy got pulled over by the police today for not stopping at a four-way stop intersection. Mommy said she did stop and got very upset with the officer, When the officer asked Mommy for her driver's license and insurance, she realized that the insurance card had expired by two days. Great........ After Mommy' and the officer "exchanged words", the officer finally gave her a warning on the traffic violation and told her to present her new card at her court date. Now this doesn't sit well with your mother. Now she has to take time away from work for a violation that she feels that she did not commit. Even if they accept her new card as valid, Mommy was told that she may still have to pay $25 for failing to have it in her possession at the time of encounter. Your Mommy and Daddy have been married for over seven years so I know that when days like these come around I say few words and walk very softly. Your mother is not happy camper right now. Myles is still the top name but the middle name is up in the air. I'm thinking ........

**Friday, October 11, 2002 (21 weeks 5 days)** The house is officially up for sale today and Mommy and Daddy are going to Mobile, Alabama to attend Mr. Walter Kimbrough's wedding (he's one of Daddy's fraternity brothers). I hope we have people come by and look at the house while we are gone. It will be great for a quick sale..... then we will be able to save more money toward the new home. It will sell on God's timetable. We will be patient.

**Friday, October 25, 2002 (23 weeks/5 days)** I apologize for waiting so late to do an entry in the journal. So many things are in the works. We are trying to work on Project Artsmart, pack up and sell the house, and organize a concert for Heartsongs (all while you are in Mommy's stomach trying to grow). Mommy has thrown up once in the last couple of weeks but she seems to have experienced a growth spurt because her stomach seems tighter. At our last checkup, the nurse said that your heart rate was around 152 beats per minute. That throws my theory out the window about boy babies have heart rates at 140 beats per minute or lower. Good thing we found out the sex or I would be a nervous wreck. It's not a secret that I wanted you to be a boy all the time. Now that we know that you're a boy I can admit that. Uncle Stephen and Auntie Joanna (your Godparents) are having another son. That will make the second boy because they already have one son named Stephen Daniel. The baby is due in early March.

There is one thing that I find strange with your mother. Mommy has found this urge to wear her hair in weird ways. Earlier this week she wore four ponytails in the front of her head with the rest hanging down in the back. Today she is wearing it with a ponytail on each side of her head (like a young child would wear her hair). She appears to be looking for reactions from her co-workers at work but she is receiving compliments rather than questions. It's frustrating her because she wants the "question" so I'm afraid she will do something real crazy for next week. Kennedi is going to the salon for the first time to have her hair done. I did not expect this until age 7 (little do I know.) I think my financial woes are starting to mount.... one good hairdo and I'm finished. She will expect her hair done every week. I wonder if McDonald's will hire a four-year-old? I can't wait until you get here. I need some help in balancing out this household.

**Tuesday, October 29, 2002 (24 weeks/2 days)** Sometimes I wonder how I'm going to attend to two kids and a wife and still have time to recharge my own battery with a little "me" time. Because Kennedi has been the only child for so long I'm not quite sure If she would transition into an older sibling role smoothly. Then there is your mother who has always jockeyed for her "quality" time. I bet she wonders whether the older ladies in my life are named XBOX and ESPN. I'm sure we will adjust..... we felt the same way when we were expecting Kennedi. We are trying to teach Kennedi how to bathe herself. Guess what, fella? I felt you move in Mommy's stomach last night. I read a website each week that tracks babies development and it says that you are now acquiring taste for sweets. Maybe that's why Mommy has been eating up all the honey buns in the pantry. Your mother has eaten so many things that she would not normally prefer if she was not pregnant. The house has not sold yet but I have faith that it will happen soon (before Christmas) Daylight savings time is killing me. It makes me sluggish because my body makes me feel like it's later than it actually is.

**Monday, November 4, 2002 (25 weeks/1 day)** It was a busy day for your mother and me. First we went to the pre-construction orientation on the new home and it went well. We were very surprised when we realized that we would get an unfinished bonus room in the floor plan. We just thought that the space was no longer existed since we opted not to add the bonus room. I admit though that it is hard to get excited about the house now when we do not know when our current home will sell. The sooner, the better is the motto. We will be very relieved when that burden is off our backs. Luckily there is plenty of time left. We also went for our monthly checkup with Dr. Sermon. Man, your heartbeat is strong!!!! The doctor said that you feel like a big baby and that everything looks fine. Next week marks the beginning of the third trimester. Mommy is still holding on to late January/early February delivery. I say you will come on time (mid - February). I'm seeing a pattern in your movement too. Every night around 11 p.m. it seems that you start kicking your mother for about an hour. Being nocturnal is not the answer in this family. Uncle Dudley and Auntie Clare are also expecting..... on February 17th (your due date). Is that wild? It would be hilarious if we were in the hospital at the same time.

**Saturday, November 9, 2002 (25 weeks/6 days)** Your cousin April came by to see us today and we went to dinner at "On the Border" in Conyers. It appears that Mommy is experiencing another growth spurt in the mid-section because you are looking bigger these days. They say that mothers tend to be bigger in their second pregnancy. We still have 14 weeks to go. I wonder if Mommy will be able to continue to work until you are born. I pray that she has the strength but it's becoming more difficult to get around.

**Monday, November 11, 2002 (26 weeks/1 day)** It is the beginning of the third trimester. This has been a very rough day for Mommy. She says that you have been moving all day and she has had a constant headache. She spent most of the night in bed.. We had chicken and noodles for dinner and Mommy seem to like it. Take it easy in there.. Yesterday was your God sister Jordyn's baby dedication. (that is your God mother's daughter) Get that? If not you will understand when you get older.

**Monday, November 25, 2002 (28 weeks/1 day)** It's getting down to the nitty-gritty and there is one person who is sooooooo excited that you are almost here. Kennedi is so excited that your due date is approaching that she hasn't even thought about Christmas. She asked us when it's December. We told her that December was only a few days away and she said "Great, now there is only two months left before my brother comes".

We had our regular checkup and Dr. Sermon's office and it appears that you are laying 'traverse' in Mommy's stomach meaning that you are sideways instead of right side up or upside down. Don't worry.... that's not a real problem. You have plenty of time to turn. Normally babies are born head first.

**Thursday, November 28, 2002 (28 weeks/4 days)** Today is Thanksgiving day. This is a time when families come together to have a big dinner and give thanks for their blessings. I'm thankful for Mommy, Kennedi, and you because you guys are the best family a man can have. Mommy is experiencing back pains that sometimes put her out of commission. She says it's just you doing somersaults in there. She says it's just you being active, but I have other ideas. I won't complain. The doctors are saying that everything is fine.

**Thursday, December 5, 2002 (29 weeks/4 days)** I don't know why but I'm feeling somewhat emotional today I can't believe that we are having a son. Sure, I see your mother's stomach and see your tosses and turns in there, but for some strange reason it hasn't hit me. Maybe because I had thought that I would have all girls since it appeared that your uncle Alex had all the boy chromosomes. I'm just proud that you have come this far. We take for granted what a child has to go through them to come into this world (without any say in the matter). Thank, God for my son. Help him to grow up to become a healthy and strong man in your Image. Help us as parents to guide him in the right direction and give him sound guidance to start his life. We love our children and thank you for these gifts...... In Jesus name. Amen.

**Wednesday, January 1 2003 (33 weeks/3 days)** Happy New Year, little man!!! Sleeping, eating and watching football is the order of business today. Of course, mommy slept in this morning but got up to put a few Christmas decorations away. Georgia beat Florida State 26-13 in the Sugar Bowl and we ragged Uncle Alex because he is a big FSU fan. I'm looking forward to another SEC championship and a trip back to the Sugar Bowl.... This time for the national championship. I can tell you may be a pretty good receiver..... you look like you may have long fingers for catching the pigskin..

**Sunday, January 12, 2003 (35 weeks)** Five weeks to D-Day and we cannot wait to see you. Especially for Mommy because it is becoming more difficult to carry you. You are getting so big. All Mommy can do when she get home is sleep because she gets tired during the day. She works an hour from home and sits behind a desk all day which is not good for the circulation. Her feet, hands, and ankles are swollen. I told her that she can stop working at any time but she wants to continue until January 31st. I have faith she knows when to say enough is enough. Mommy's friends had a baby shower and you got a lot of goodies for your arrival. God has truly blessed us because we gave most of our baby stuff away once Kennedi reached toddler age. Mommy is having another baby shower this weekend from her co-workers. You are racking up, boy!!!!

**Monday, January 13, 2003 (35 weeks/1 day)** Mommy and I went to her routine check-up at Dr. Sermons office. The nurse joked with her about how big her stomach was and guessed that you were about over five pounds at this stage of the pregnancy. Dr. Sermon suggested that Mommy could decide to schedule your birth in 2 weeks. At first Mommy was excited about the idea but later thought that it would be in the best interest to let nature take its course. We also have some encouraging news about the house: We received an offer from a potential buyer. Although Mommy and I believe the initial offer is too low, we believe that it is a good starting point.

**Monday, January 27, 2003 (37 weeks 1 day)** Today is a routine check-up to see how you are doing. Dr. Sermon just squeezed Mommy's stomach a bit to check your position and gave her a clean bill of health. The nurse is at the office are amazed at how big you appear. Dr. Sermon says that he would guess that you are over seven pounds... WOW!!! You still have three weeks left. The house is still up for sale without a contract. Most people that call about the house are looking to rent or lease purchase the house. We have to pray about this because this is not our preferred option. By the way, Super Bowl XXXVII was played last night. Tampa Bay Buccaneers 49, Oakland Raiders 21. President Bush is delivering his State of Union address tomorrow to tell the nation the likelihood of war with Iraq. The economy is also shot!!! It may explain why the house has been on the market for nearly four months. I keep telling myself, let tomorrow worry about itself; focus on today. God has something powerful in store for us. We will keep trusting in Him.

**Wednesday, January 29, 2003 (37 weeks /3 days)** We're getting down to the crunch time now. In less than three weeks, you will be here on this Earth. Today Uncle Dudley and Auntie Claire had their third son, Hollis Langston White. Obviously he beat you to the punch and decided to make an early appearance. You and Hollis were due on the same day (February 17th) I guess you like being in the womb more than he did. I think Mommy has thoughts of inducing labor if you are not here by next weekend. She tends and go back and forth on things. It's understandable.... It must be hard to carry all the extra weight around.

**Friday, January 31, 2003 (37 weeks/5 days)** Today is Mommy's last working day at the Corban Group and I am excited for her. She has accomplished her goal to make it to the end of the month. Many say that she will probably go into labor now that she can finally relax... Right!!! You know what relaxation is. She thinks she can do all things she normally does but it's a struggle with swollen feet/hands, sore back, baby kicks in the ribs and vital organs, baby stretches, fatigue. You name it..... Mommy has experienced it all with this pregnancy.

**Monday, February 3, 2003 (38 weeks/1 day)** We went to our weekly doctor's appointment with the hope that Dr. Sermon would recommend that we induce labor by this weekend. That didn't happen. The good news is that mommy has dilated 1 centimeter. The only way that he would agree to induce would be if Mommy tested positive for toxemia. We will know the results of that test by Wednesday. Will you come on already?

**Wednesday, February 5, 2003 ( 38 weeks /3 Days)** Mommy is officially at the miserable state right now and you seem to be so content to stay in there. Every step for her is painful and she just wants you out. I think active labor would be a welcome change for her right now. As you will learn, your mother likes to be on the go and when there is something (or someone) that impedes her ability to do so she becomes unnerved to the point of utter frustration, which causes her to tense up. I think she is at that point and I need for her to relax but I don't know how to help her relax. We are both anxious for you to be born. I guess I need to calm myself so I can help her. In an ironic way the labor pain will bring a sigh of relief. If I didn't know any better, l would think you were waiting to come on my birthday.

By the way, there is a baby pool at my job predicting when you will be born and at what weight. Currently there are two ladies on the clock. - Elizabeth (February 7th 8 lb. and 8 oz) and Janice (February 7th 8 lb. and 2 oz).

**Sunday, February 9, 2003 (39 weeks)** After breaking off negotiations with the first and only person to offer on the house, I felt that God led me to call her back to resume talk. To make a long story short, your Mommy and I were discussing a fair price for the house about 3 weeks ago but we felt that the offer price was too low. We felt that the offer would not provide us with the desire return of our investment in the house, but something in my spirit was telling me that this was the right person to assume ownership of the house. In obedience to my spirit I left a voice message for the buyer to call us back. I do not know where this is going to lead. I guess that it is essence of faith.

**Monday, February 10, 2003 (39 weeks/1 day)** The buyer return our call today and said that she is still interested in resuming negotiations to buy the house. That's the best news we've had in months. We have had several people inquire about the property but nothing serious. I'm trying not to focus on the money aspect of this deal and trust God to meet with that need from other sources. Mommy and I are committed to making this work for both sides because the buyer is in desperate need of a home and we are in a desperate need to move (the new home is scheduled to close in six weeks). This is what we are focusing on and pray that God will take care of the rest.

We had our weekly visit with Dr. Sermon today. He checked Mommy but there has not been much progress from last week, Mommy was somewhat discouraged hoping that she would have dilated a little more but she realizes that the main thing was that you were happy and safe. On the way home Mommy and I discussed the possibility of her taking castor oil to induce labor. Considering all the pain she has experienced over the several months this didn't sound like a bad option. She later decided to wait it out a little longer.

**Tuesday, February 11, 2003 (39 weeks/2 days)** Mommy and Kennedi have been joking that you will come on my birthday, but I knew better. You ain't trying to come out of there. Today is your father's 34th birthday and the good news of the day is that I believe that we are closer to having a contract placed to sell our house. We will know if it's official by the end of the day. That will be the greatest birthday present I could receive right now because I am weary of the strain. I feel like I have been pulled in many directions - taking care of you and Mommy, giving enough time to Kennedi, packing up the house, and tending to affairs with the new house. I'm tired and I want you to come and all this house stuff be over. Maybe God takes us to a certain point where we feel that we have ended all of our energies and say, "Please, help me" that's when He says my "grace is sufficient." I have come to realize that the faith walk is not always pretty but it's always ends up for our benefit. Got to go and pack up the kitchen. This moving stuff is no joke.

**Wednesday, February 12, 2003 (39 weeks 3 days)** Well, we did it!!!! We finally found someone to buy the house. Her name is Sharon Burnette and she has a daughter named Jade (age 7) Mommy, Kennedi and I are so happy because the hardest part is over. Her schedule time to move into the house is March 28th. Now let's pray for three things; that we close on this house on time, that we close on the new house on time (March 31$^{st}$), and that you come soon. Sunday will be the 40th week and your mother is tired. Will you come already? God may not come when you want him but he's always on time. This experience has been a testament to that fact.

Mommy has been complaining about what she believes are minor cramps. Hopefully it will progress into full labor. I'm getting a little antsy about your arrival.

**Saturday, February 15, 2003 (39 weeks 6 days)** Almost a week from the original due date and we are traveling in uncharted territory (Kennedi was born 4 weeks early). I woke up this morning with a mission to have an active day planned for Mommy because we were determined to have you this weekend. So, Mommy, Kennedy and I left the house early to get breakfast and went Furniture shopping. We must have stopped out of half a dozen stores looking for a kitchen set and a bed for Kennedi. All day we walked around the different stores so Mommy could get her exercise. (It is believed that walking may induce labor). I even tried running over every pothole and railroad tracks I found to cause labor. I heard that spicy foods may do the trick too so I ordered Mommy some jerk chicken. Since she was on the spicy food crave she didn't mind the gesture at all. I was praying that the combination of all these tricks would start labor.

**Sunday, February 16, 2003 (40 weeks)** approximately 2:30 a.m.
I wake up to long moaning's from the other side of the bed. Mommy was complaining about pains slightly stronger than the normal Braxton-Hicks she had experienced off and on for the past four weeks. I immediately got up and put my contacts in to start timing the contractions. For the first hour, contractions were approximately five minutes away. Maybe all the walking and spicy foods on Saturday did the trick I think you may be on your way--- finally.

As daybreak approached, the contractions begin to remain about four to five minutes apart. I made breakfast for Mommy and got Kennedi up to take her to Pam's house. (If you read this first journal for Kennedi's birth you will know that I made one waffle before she went to the hospital and she was hungry later that day because the hospital only gives ice chips during labor) We left the house around 8:45 a.m. on our way to the hospital.

**Around 9:45 a.m.**
We arrived at Northside Hospital and checked into the Maternity Ward. Auntie Lorraine arrived at the hospital shortly afterwards. Mommy had been consistently experiencing contractions three to four minutes apart for 30 seconds in duration. After checking Mommy's condition, the nurse told her that she had only dilated 1 cm and wanted to consult with Dr. Sermons to determine whether she should go home until she thins out more. Despite the low dilation reading all factors indicated that Mommy was nearing active labor and now it would be a waiting game at the painful expense of your mother. Dr. Sermons agreed and authorize her to stay in the hospital. Once again, your mother was a trooper with her breathing.


**Around 11:15 a.m.**
Mommy is very tired now because she's been contracting for at least nine hours (maybe longer because that was the time I woke up to her moaning.  She could have been cramping before then) the nurses are checking up on mommy every fifteen minutes and the latest dilation reading was four centimeters (three centimeters more from the initial reading). Things are progressing but Mommy is struggling. She is not too far from the epidural but I believe she will have to labor a little while longer.

**Around 12:30 p.m.**
Mommy has received the epidural and is now snoring. Like her labor with Kennedi, contractions are registering off the scale but Mommy is knocked out. Hopefully we will have a welcome surprise by the time she wakes up and you will finally decide to come out there. By this time, Auntie Pat has come by to visit. Auntie Pat is one of your late Grandma Beryl best friends. For a brief moment it brought back memories of when Grandma Beryl was there when Mommy was having Kennedi. Since Auntie Pat is also a nurse (like Grandma Beryl) she would attend to Mommy between nurses visit (adjust the heart rate monitor around Mommy's stomach, adjust her position in the bed, etc.) I'm sure Mommy had the same thoughts and longings for her mother to be there but for some strange feeling I believe she was there the whole time-- in spirit. I thank God for Auntie Pat because she was a tremendous support and filling a void Auntie Lorraine nor I could fill for Mommy at this point – motherly like care. Thank you Mom for being there.

## Around 1:20 p.m.

Mommy was still in active labor (11 hour started from the time I woke up) and she has dilated six centimeter. Suddenly Mommy's and your condition took a critical turn. During the nurses routine check, she obviously noticed a sudden drop. After she barked several orders over the intercom, a core of nurses rushed into the room to assist. It was chaos and my heart rate tripled the normal rate. "What's going on?" I'm saying to myself. The nurse hurriedly placed an oxygen mask over Mommy's nose. Auntie Pat calmly instructed Mommy to breathe deeply into the mask. I saw the sudden concern on Mommy's face over the commotion but sensed her composure to simply do as Auntie Pat instructed. As for me, I felt totally helpless. Here I am coaching my wife to maintain her breathing for eleven hours and then be faced with the fact that something is going bad wrong. Will our son be OK? As I continued to encourage Mommy that everything is fine my spirit is fervently praying for safety, comfort, and peace for my wife and son. It was like I could feel the spiritual war raging inside my soul. My flesh wanted to fear the worst but my spirit was at total peace. I knew everything would be fine but the thoughts of doubt and fear was trying to invade my psyche.

## Around 1:45 p.m.

By this time I have lost all track of time. It was explained to me that your heart rate had decreased significantly in a short amount of time. You were having problems getting in the birth position (head first) because you were tangled up in the umbilical cord (once around your neck, once around your arms and once around the waist). The contractions were trying to push you out: the cord was holding you back. Because you were so tangled up in there, the doctor ordered that your mother undergo an emergency C-section. This is a process when the baby is taken out through the stomach instead of the vagina (the birth canal). I was ordered to put on hospital clothes and wait outside the emergency room until the doctor's finished preparing your mother for surgery. It felt like I sat there forever but in hindsight it was only a few minutes. For some strange reason I felt that everything would be alright even though I knew that they had not taken you out of mommy's stomach yet. I was still praying for deliverance because I knew it was nothing I could do on my own accord.

**Around 2 p.m.**
I am with Mommy now and I expected her to be sedated by now….NO. She is wide awake and be very uncooperative. I had to literally hold her down and try to calm her because she is panicking and very upset. I do not blame her because all she knows both of your lives were at stake. Even at her worst time of least composure (which I would have to say this is #1 on the list) she did a much better job than If it was me on the table. First of all I HATE HOSPITALS with a passion. If I was the mother and Mommy was the father consider yourself blessed because neither you nor Kennedi would be here. I would not have children. It takes great courage to birth a child.

When the anesthesia finally took effect, things begin to calm down in the room. After I while I heard a small cry from the other end of the operating table. I could not see beyond your mother's waist so I could only hear you. Your cry was a joy to my soul. I kept telling your mother, I hear him…… I hear him" to comfort her.

**At 2:30 p.m.**
You were born *Myles Erickson Smith*    7 lbs. 7 oz 21 in long. After a few moments, I was allowed to hold you and all I could see was your mother's face. Man, you took some detours to get here but you finally made it. The doctors had to resuscitate you at birth. You are indeed a miracle child. Like Kennedi, your mother and I promise to provide you with all the love, joy, and opportunity that life has to offer.

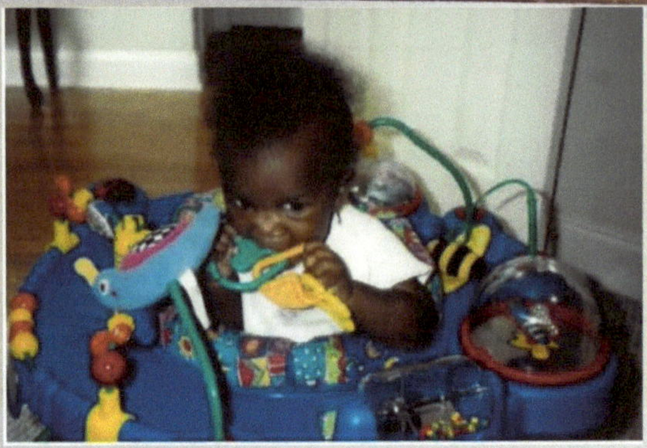

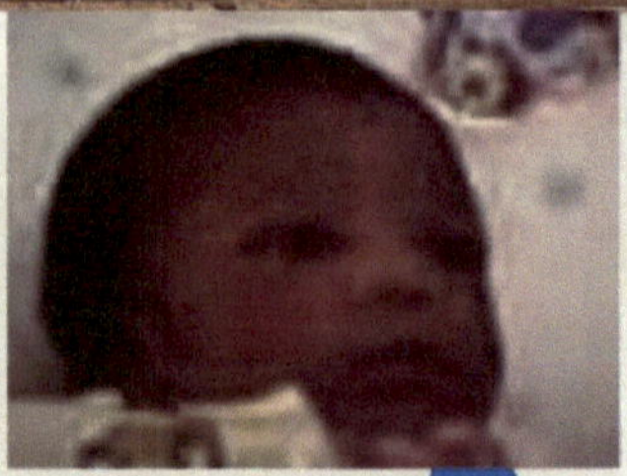

# Myles

This Journal reveals more information about our pregnancy cycles. It highlights all the ups and downs of pregnancy and labor while showing the mindset of our father and how he was feeling. We hope that we served at least half of what our father's dream vision of a family was from June of 1997. Now, twenty three years later, we hope we can build on that and fulfill the vision of the future of our family.

NGRATS
NNEDI
3S 07 20
CO.
KE
CLAS
CO.
KE
AS.
ATHENS
GEORGIA
OKLAHOMA
CITY
0
adidas
LAS VEGAS

2
KODAK PORTA 400
2

2
KODAK PORTA 400
2

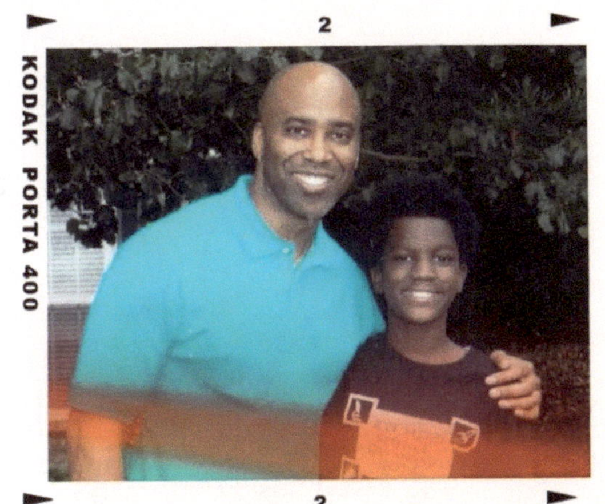

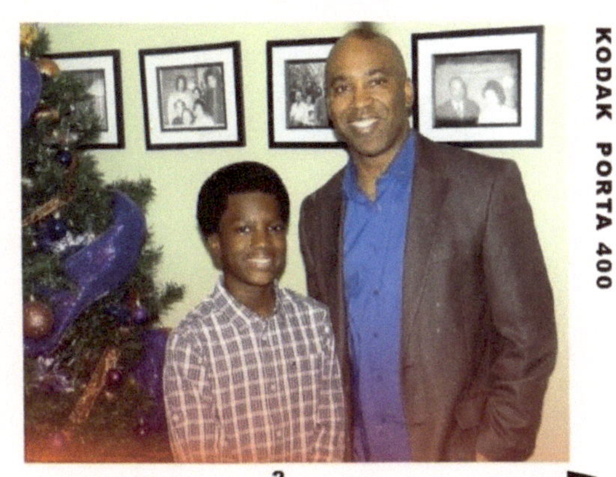

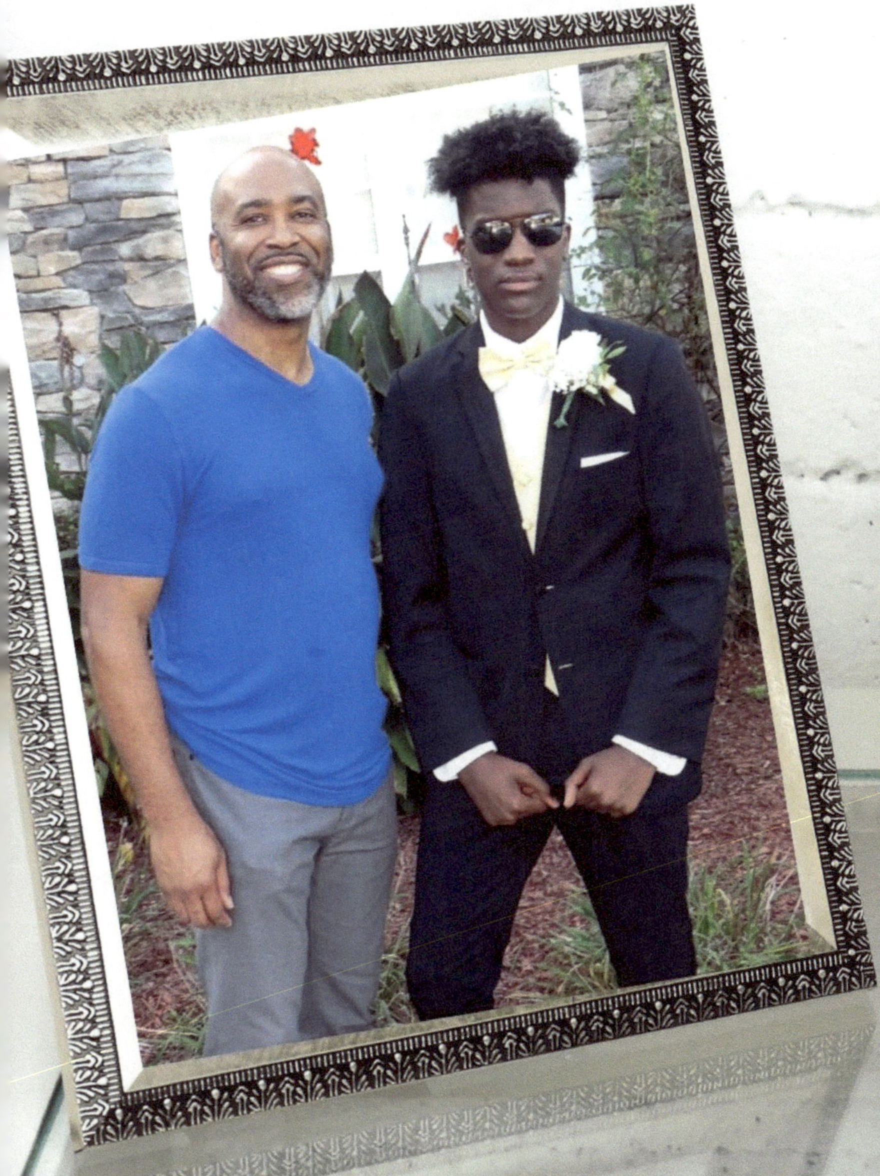

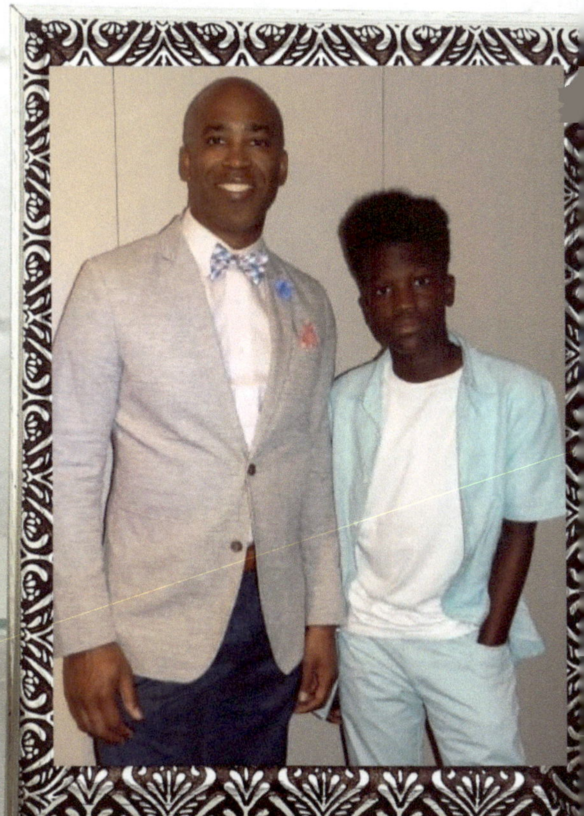

2000

2001

2002

2003

2004

2005

2006

2007

2008

2009

2010

2011

2012

2013

2014

2015

2016

love

## About the Author

Keith Erickson Smith lives in
Lilburn, Georgia with his wife, Heather and two children,
Kennedi and Myles.
Keith is a dual graduate of the University of Georgia where he
received a Bachelor's degree in Political Science and a
Master's degree in Public Administration. Keith can rival any
political commentator with his love and passion for
politics. He enjoys playing golf, watching sports, cooking and
spending time with his family. Keith is also an active member
of Alpha Phi Alpha Fraternity, Inc.
"Daddy's Journals" reveal some of his most intimate thoughts
as he prepared to parent his two children. With God at the
center of his family, Keith has been an amazing father for
twenty-two years and counting.
To contact Keith, please email him at
**www.daddysjournals.com**